SPORTS
Machines

Snowmobiles

By E. S. Budd

The Child's World®

Published by The Child's World®
PO Box 326
Chanhassen, MN 55317-0326
800-599-READ
www.childsworld.com

Design and Production:
The Creative Spark, San Juan Capistrano, CA

Photo Credits: Images on pages 5 and 8 courtesy of Polaris Sales, Medina, Minnesota.
Images on pages 6, 13 (inset), 16, and 17 courtesy of HughesPhoto.com.
All other images ©2003 David M. Budd Photography.

Library of Congress Cataloging-in-Publication Data

Budd, E. S.
  Snowmobiles / by E.S. Budd.
      p. cm. — (Sport machines at work)
Summary: Introduces the recreational use of snowmobiles, safety tips,
and competitive racing, including snowcross.
  ISBN 1-59296-165-7 (Library Bound : alk. paper)
 1. Snowmobiling—Juvenile literature. 2. Snowmobiling—Safety
measures—Juvenile literature. [1. Snowmobiling. 2. Snowmobiles.] I. Title.
  GV856.5.B83 2004
  796.94—dc22
                                200302139

Contents

Let's Go Snowmobiling!

Snowmobiles are a great way to travel across snow and ice. Each winter more than four million American and Canadian riders enjoy the outdoors on their snowmobiles. Riders can travel places they couldn't reach on foot or by car.

The first snowmobiles were like motorized sleds. They helped people in snowy places get to town for supplies. In an emergency, snowmobiles could save lives. Doctors, veterinarians, and ambulance drivers used them in their work. Soon people realized a snowmobile could be fun, too.

Snowmobiles used to be much bigger. They could seat up to 12 people. Later, smaller ones were built. They could move much more quickly.

Some riders go snowmobiling on trails located close to home. Others make snowmobiling part of their vacation time. They load their snowmobiles onto trailers to get to the best places for the sport.

On a snowmobile, you can see some of the most beautiful places in the world. You can tour forests and national parks—such as Yellowstone in Wyoming or Voyageurs in Minnesota. You can enjoy exciting places like Alaska's Denali National Park.

There are snowmobile trails in almost every state—and Canada, too! In North America alone, there are about 225,000 miles of snowmobile trails.

It's important to stay on safe, well-maintained trails. Accidents are most likely to happen when people ride in unsafe places. Hidden rocks or fences, low-hanging branches, and tree stumps are just a few of the hazards that riders may encounter. Hitting an icy patch at high speed is another danger. Avalanches are a hazard when traveling into the back country. Riders need to check with local authorities to find out where it's safe to snowmobile. Forest service workers and volunteers **groom** the trails and clearly mark hazards so they are visible.

Snowmobiling is a sport for people of all ages—from young children to grandparents. At first children ride with adults. They can also race mini snowmobiles, called Kitty Cats, like the blue one shown at right. Once they are old enough, kids can drive a snowmobile all by themselves. They can even take their friends for a ride. It's easy to learn to drive a snowmobile!

13

Snowmobile riders know it's important to think about safety. Both kids and adults wear helmets with visors or goggles. Gloves, sturdy boots, and snowsuits keep people protected and warm. A backpack can carry a first-aid kit, food, and other supplies.

Safe riders never drive too fast or too close to another snowmobile. They always tell someone where they are going—especially when traveling to remote areas.

For the best riders, snowmobiling is a competitive sport. Snowcross is the most popular form of snowmobile racing. Riders compete on a track with tight turns and jumps, often catching air as they race to the finish line at top speeds. Ice racing is another extreme sport for top-notch riders.

Most people snowmobile for fun, but
these vehicles serve other functions, too.
In some places, snowmobiles are people's
main source of transportation. Police and
other officials use snowmobiles for
search-and-rescue work and to move
quickly and safely in snowy conditions.

Forest workers and scientists use them to travel into the woods during the winter. The ski patrol uses snowmobiles to rescue injured skiers and to help keep ski trails safe. Snowmobiles can tow sleds behind them to transport people to safety or carry supplies.

Climb Aboard!

Would you like to see what it's like to go snowmobiling? Riders use handlebars to control their snowmobiles. The **throttle** and **brake** are on the handlebars. The throttle speeds up the snowmobile, and the brake slows it down. Some snowmobiles even have heated grips on the handlebars to keep the driver's hands warm. In an emergency, the driver can push the kill switch to shut off the engine quickly. A speedometer tells drivers how fast they are going.

1. Handlebars
2. Throttle
3. Brake
4. Kill switch
5. Speedometer

Up Close

Snowmobiles have **skis** and **tracks.** The handlebars steer the skis to help the vehicle glide across the snow. The skis also help to stabilize the snowmobile. The engine powers the track, which is a wide, rubber belt with treads called **lugs.** The lugs grip the snow for **traction.** The track **propels** the snowmobile through the snow.

1. Skis
2. Track
3. Handlebars
4. Engine
5. Lugs

Glossary

brake (BRAYK) A brake is a control on a snowmobile. It helps the rider stop or slow down.

groom (GROOM) To groom a trail means to smooth it and prepare it for use by removing hazards. Forest workers and volunteers groom trails to make them safer.

lugs (LUGZ) Lugs are part of the track on a snowmobile. They grip the snow and provide traction.

propels (pro-PELLZ) To propel is to drive something forward. The track propels a snowmobile.

skis (SKEEZ) Skis are part of a snowmobile. A snowmobile has two skis that help to steer and stabilize it.

throttle (THRAWT-ull) A throttle is a control on a snowmobile. It helps riders control how fast they go.

tracks (TRAKS) A track is part of a snowmobile. It is a wide, rubber belt powered by the engine that propels the snowmobile.

traction (TRAK-shun) Traction is friction that helps to move a vehicle forward and keep it from sliding. The lugs on a snowmobile provide traction.